MIDNIGHT BABIES

BY MARGARET WILD
ILLUSTRATED BY ANN JAMES

CLARION BOOKS
NEW YORK

For Morag — M.W.

For sweet baby Andie James — A.J.

Clarion Books
a Houghton Mifflin Company imprint
215 Park Avenue South, New York, NY 10003

First published in 1999 in Australia by ABC Books for the Australian
Broadcasting Corporation, GPO Box 9994, Sydney, NSW 2001.
First published in the United States in 2001.

The illustrations were drawn with chalk pastels on colored paper.
The text was set in Garamond Bold.
Designed and typeset by Monkeyfish.

For information about permission to reproduce selections from this
book, write to Permissions, Houghton Mifflin Company,
215 Park Avenue South, New York, NY 10003.

www.houghtonmifflinbooks.com

Printed in Hong Kong.

Library of Congress Cataloging-in-Publication Data

Wild, Margaret, 1948 –
Midnight babies / by Margaret Wild; illustrated by Ann James.
p. cm.
Summary: Baby Brenda and her friends have fun at the Midnight Café,
enjoying a "wibble wobble" dance, a "jiggly-joggly" treat, and a dip in the
sprinklers before going home to bed.
ISBN 0-618-10412-7
[1. Babies – Fiction.] I. James, Ann, ill. II. Title

PZ7.W64574 Mg 2001
[E] – dc21   00-058978

10 9 8 7 6 5 4 3 2 1

At midnight, when absolutely anything can happen,
Baby Brenda bounces out of bed.

She tiptoes past her sleeping mom and dad,

does a dance outside her big sister Vanessa's room,

then slides down the stairs to the kitchen.

Baby Brenda opens the refrigerator.
"Yum!" she says, and fills up her backpack with goodies.

Then Baby Brenda wriggles through the cat door.
Her friends are waiting for her, with a BIG surprise—
a jiggly-joggly treat.

Brenda and her friends
race out of the garden,
up the road,
and around the corner
to their favorite place,
the Midnight Café.

But . . .

Baby Mario and his friends are already there!
"Hrrumph!" says Baby Brenda.
"Hrrumph!" say her friends.
Baby Mario scowls, and so do *his* friends.

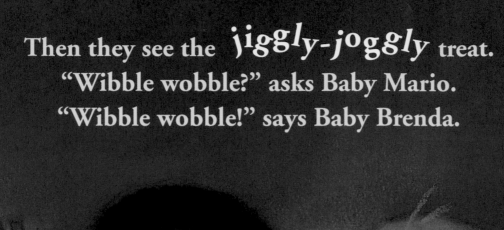

Then they see the jiggly-joggly treat.
"Wibble wobble?" asks Baby Mario.
"Wibble wobble!" says Baby Brenda.

Blibble Blobble!

Blibble Blobble!

Whirly-whirl!
All fall down!

Phew!

The babies are so hungry they're ready to feast . . .
and feast . . .
and FEAST!

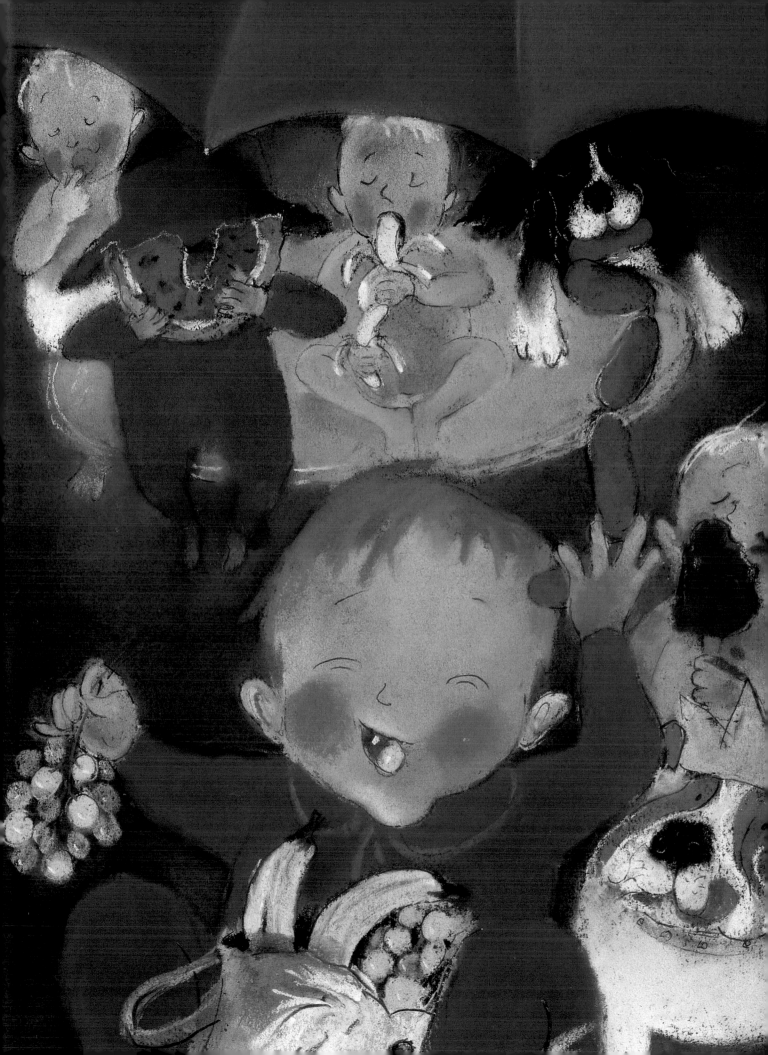

Last of all, they eat the **jiggly-joggly** treat.

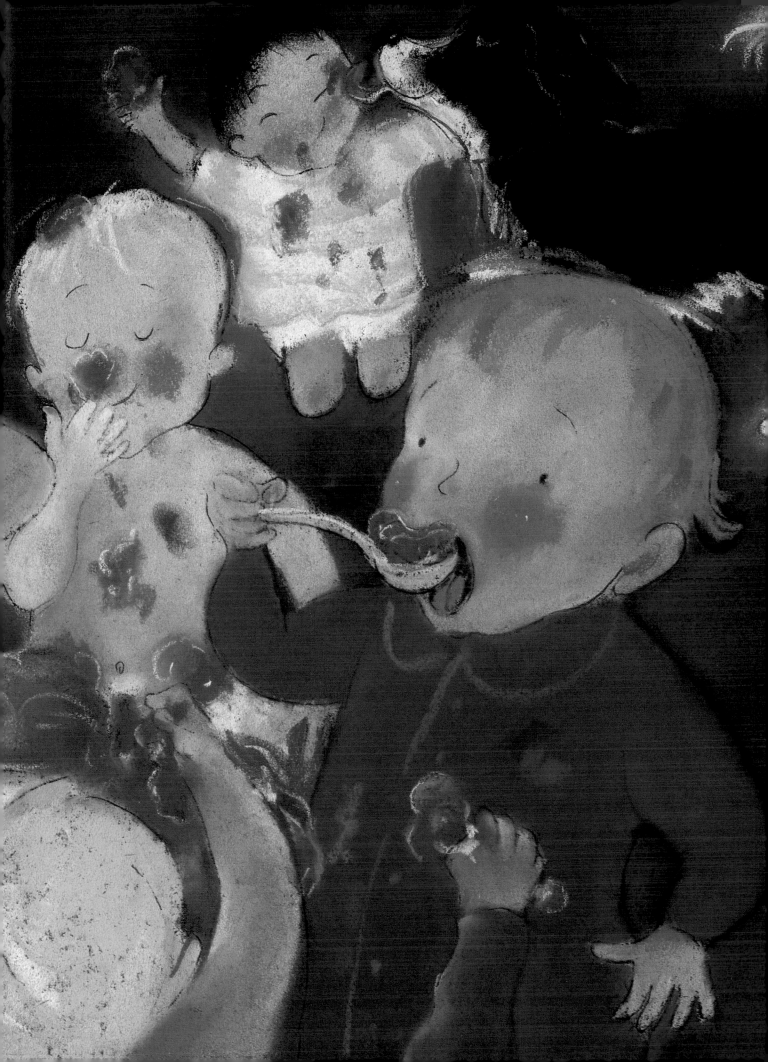

When there's nothing left of the jiggly-joggly treat
—not a blib, not a blob—
they play dress-up with the food.
Baby Brenda thinks Baby Mario looks dashing!
And Baby Mario thinks Baby Brenda looks divine!

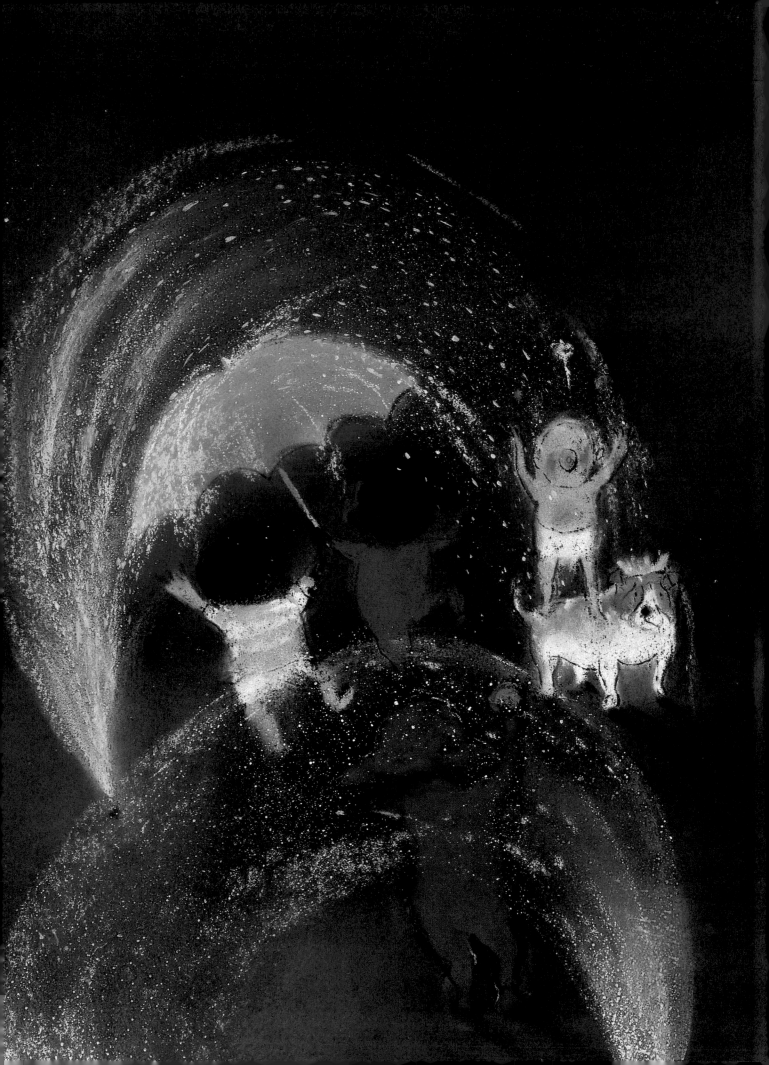

Just before the sun comes up,
the babies go for a dip
under the sprinklers.

Then they say good-bye, and waddle home.

Baby Brenda gets stuck in the cat door for a while,

then crawls up the stairs,

and flops into bed.

That morning at breakfast, Baby Brenda can't eat a thing.
"Just have an itty-bitty spoonful,"
says her big sister Vanessa.

Baby Brenda clamps her mouth shut.
"Poor little Brenda," says Vanessa. "If you don't eat up,
you won't grow big and strong like me!"

**But Baby Brenda just
pats her fat little tummy,
tips her bowl of cereal over her head—
and _burrrps_!**